A NOTE TO PARENTS

Early Step into Reading Books are designed for preschoolers and kindergartners who are just getting ready to read. The words are easy, the type is big, and the stories are packed with rhyme, rhythm, and repetition.

We suggest that you read this book to your child the first few times, pointing to each word as you go. Soon your child will start saying the words with you. And before long, he or she will try to read the story alone. Don't be surprised if your child uses the pictures to figure out the text—that's what they're there for! The important thing is to develop your child's confidence—and to show your child that reading is fun.

When your child is ready to move on, try the rest of the steps in our Step into Reading series. **Step 1 Books** (preschool–grade 1) feature the same easy-to-read type as the Early Step into Reading Books, but with more words per page. **Step 2 Books** (grades 1–3) are both longer and slightly more difficult, while **Step 3 Books** (grades 2–3) introduce readers to paragraphs and fully developed plot lines. **Step 4 Books** (grades 2–4) offer exciting nonfiction for the increasingly independent reader.

For Jim, with love
—L. H.

To: Tiffany, Scampi,
Cheyenne, Angie, Chili,
Maggie, Calvin & Chuck
—J. M.

Random House 🏠 New York

Text copyright © 1998 by Lori Haskins. Illustrations copyright © 1998 by Joe Mathieu.
All rights reserved under International and Pan-American Copyright Conventions.
Published in the United States by Random House, Inc., New York, and simultaneously
in Canada by Random House of Canada Limited, Toronto.
http://www.randomhouse.com/

Library of Congress Cataloging-in-Publication Data
Haskins, Lori.
Too many dogs / by Lori Haskins ; illustrated by Joe Mathieu.
p. cm. — (Early step into reading)
SUMMARY: A man's barbecue is interrupted when it is visited by a bevy of
dogs from the neighborhood.
ISBN 0-679-86443-1 (pbk.) — ISBN 0-679-96443-6 (lib. bdg.)
[1. Dogs—Fiction.] I. Mathieu, Joe, ill. II. Title. III. Series.
PZ7.H27645To 1998 [E]—dc20 95-7899
Printed in the United States of America 10 9 8 7 6 5 4 3 2 1

EARLY STEP INTO READING is a trademark of Random House, Inc.

TOO MANY DOGS

BY LORI HASKINS

ILLUSTRATED BY JOE MATHIEU

Big dog.

Bigger dog.

Biggest dog of all.

Small dog.

Smaller dog.

Smallest of the small.

Waggy dog.

Shaggy dog.

Doggies in a bunch.

Floppy dog.

Sloppy dog.

Doggies eating lunch!

Sprinkly dog.
Wrinkly dog.

Scratchy dog.

Patchy dog.

Tricky dog.

Picky dog.

Happy, lappy, licky dog!

Spotty dog.

Dotty dog.

Doggies all about.

Howly dog.

Growly dog.

Doggies, please get OUT!

WOOF!